For Georgie and Conrad
   ~L.J.

For Even, with love
   ~J.M.

First published in the United States 1997 by
Little Tiger Press, N16 W23390 Stoneridge Drive,
Waukesha, WI 53188
Originally published in Great Britain 1997 by
Magi Publications, London
Text © 1997 Linda Jennings
Illustrations © 1997 Julia Malim
All rights reserved.
Library of Congress Cataloging-in-Publication Data
Jennings, Linda.
Lonely Misty / by Linda Jennings;   pictures by Julia Malim.
p.   cm.
Summary : Unhappy because her kittens have been
given away, Misty seeks comradeship among the barn cats,
returns to the house, and finds that someone has
followed her home.
ISBN 1-888444-21-5
1. Cats—Juvenile fiction. [1. Cats—Fiction.]
I. Malim, Julia, 1955–   ill. II. Title.
PZ10.3.J429Lo 1997 [E]—dc21 97-16837 CIP AC
Printed in Belgium
First American Edition
1 3 5 7 9 10 8 6 4 2

Lonely Misty

by Linda Jennings

Pictures by Julia Malim

Misty woke up feeling cold.

All her kittens had gone to new homes, and she missed their warm, furry bodies curled up beside her. It was wintertime, and the sky was the color of slate. Misty looked through the window and saw tiny snowflakes whirling around in the wind.

Misty remembered what fun she'd had playing with her kittens. She knew they would leave eventually—kittens became cats after all, and house cats needed lots of space. They were excited about having new adventures in new places. But Misty missed them and often wondered about Jasper, the littlest. He had seemed quite happy where he was. He hadn't wanted to go to his new home.

In the living room Misty's family was busy, and they didn't notice her at first. She wound herself around their legs and meowed. When she tried to help Polly wrap a birthday present, Polly got angry. "Misty, look what you've done!" she said. "I'll *never* be ready for Sam's party now. You are a pest."

Misty banged her way out through
the cat flap. She felt very unwanted.

Misty crossed the silent yard and leaped onto
the wall, where she sat watching a family of foxes
playing in the frozen field.

She thought some more about her kittens.
She imagined taking them on hunts through the
woods and visiting the big barn. Finally it got cold
on the wall, and Misty jumped down and made her
way toward the barn.

In the woods it was very quiet and still, and there was no snow under the thick pine trees. As Misty padded along the frosty path, she thought she heard something. It sounded like a kitten crying. She listened again, but there was only the wind in the treetops. Misty reached the edge of the woods, where she could just see the barn across the field.

Usually the barn cats cheered Misty up with their long stories about rat chases and hayloft hunts. But today their tales didn't interest her. She kept thinking that nobody took barn cats to new homes. Farm cats and kittens lived together their whole lives, and they never got lonely. They laughed at Misty when she told them she heard a kitten crying in the woods.

Misty stayed in the barn all day.
When the barn cats finally got tired of
pouncing on one another and went to sleep,
Misty felt the cold creep over her from the
tips of her ears to the pads of her feet.
Though the farm cats knew her well, they
didn't ask her to curl up with them.

It was time to go home, and Misty crept out
of the barn and into a snowy, white world.
    The wind blew across the field and through
the trees, and to Misty it still sounded like a lost
kitten meowing.

Misty was hungry and looked forward to
sleeping in front of a nice, warm fire. She tried
to think about her catnip mouse and her
scratching post instead of kittens.

Down through the yard Misty padded. Her paws sank into the snow, making fresh prints. It was dark now, and the yard was full of moonlight and shadows. One of the shadows seemed to move across the lawn behind Misty as she went through the cat flap.

"Oh, there you are," said Mom,
picking Misty up and giving her a hug.
"I've got some tuna for your dinner
tonight." Misty purred and almost
forgot about kittens for a moment.
"What's that noise?" said Dad.
"I thought I heard something outside."
He went to open the door.

There on the step sat a wet,
bedraggled kitten with huge eyes.
It was Jasper!

Misty ran to Jasper, purring loudly.

"What a sight he is!" cried Dad. "I wonder why he's come home."

Mom put down a big saucer of tuna, and Misty let Jasper eat most of it.

"Can we keep him?" pleaded Polly. "*Please?*"

    While Misty cleaned Jasper from tip to tail with her rough tongue, Dad called his owners. "Well, it seems Jasper and their baby didn't get along so well," he said, hanging up the phone. "They'd be just as happy if we kept him."

    Later that night, Jasper told his mother how he'd missed her so much that he'd run away. When he reached the woods, he had seen Misty and followed her home.

Jasper soon fell asleep against his mother's warm side. "Tomorrow I'll show him off to the barn cats," Misty thought. With Jasper home, she was happy at last.